GAME ON!
SUPER RABBIT BOY!

LOOK OUT FOR MORE ADVENTURES WITH SUPER RABBIT BOY!

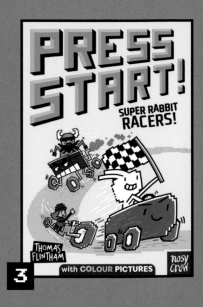

PRESS START!

GAME ON, SUPER RABBIT BOY!

THOMAS FLINTHAM

nosy crow

FOR JACK

First published as *Game Over, Super Rabbit Boy!*
in the United States in 2016 by Scholastic Inc
This edition published in the UK in 2023 by Nosy Crow Ltd
The Crow's Nest, 14 Baden Place,
Crosby Row, London, SE1 1YW, UK

Nosy Crow Eireann Ltd
44 Orchard Grove, Kenmare,
Co Kerry, V93 FY22, Ireland

Nosy Crow and associated logos are trademarks and/or registered
trademarks of Nosy Crow Ltd

Copyright © Thomas Flintham, 2016

The right of Thomas Flintham to be identified as the
author and illustrator of this work has been asserted by him
in accordance with the Copyright, Designs and Patents Act 1988.

Printed and bound in China.

Papers used by Nosy Crow are made from wood grown in sustainable forests.

1 3 5 7 9 10 8 6 4 2

www.nosycrow.com

TABLE OF
CONTENTS

This is Animal Town.

SUPER FUNSTON

START

SELECT

It is a peaceful town full of happy animal friends. The townspeople have fun all the time. They play games. They dance. They have a party every day.

This is Singing Dog. He lives in Animal Town. He loves happiness. He loves fun. And he loves to make other people happy. Everyone has fun with Singing Dog. Singing Dog really knows how to be happy!

Singing Dog

This is King Viking. He lives in Boom Boom Factory high up on Mount Boom. He does not like happiness. He does not like fun. And he really does not like other people who are happy and fun. Not one bit.

King Viking

King Viking can't stand the fun going on in Animal Town. He has never danced. He has never played games. He has only ever been mean! So he has come up with a No-Fun Plan.

King Viking and his Robot Army travel across the land. They travel from Boom Boom Factory all the way to Animal Town.

The townspeople run away in fear when they see King Viking. Everyone knows he is mean and horrible. He brings trouble with him everywhere.

Oh no! Singing Dog is too busy singing and dancing. He doesn't see King Viking and his Robot Army!

King Viking grabs Singing Dog and ties him up.

King Viking rushes back to Boom Boom Factory. But he leaves his robots behind.

3 SUPER RABBIT BOY!

Simon the Hedgehog runs as fast as his legs can carry him. He runs all the way to Carrot Castle.

Then the greatest hero of all time steps out of the castle: Super Rabbit Boy!

Flashback . . .

WHEN HE WAS ONLY A BABY, RABBIT BOY CRAWLED TO THE WOODS TO FIND SOMETHING TO EAT.

BUT HE FELL THROUGH A HOLE INTO A VERY SPECIAL BONUS MAZE LEVEL.

AFTER A LONG, HUNGRY SEARCH, RABBIT BOY FOUND A SHINY SUPER CARROT IN THE CENTRE OF THE MAZE. IT LOOKED VERY TASTY. RABBIT BOY GULPED IT UP IN ONE BITE!

BUT IT WAS NO ORDINARY CARROT. IT WAS A SUPER MAGICAL CARROT!

FROM THAT DAY FORWARDS, WHENEVER RABBIT BOY ATE A SUPER MAGICAL CARROT, HE COULD JUMP REALLY HIGH ...

... AND RUN REALLY, REALLY FAST! (EVEN FASTER THAN SIMON THE HEDGEHOG!)

HE WAS THE STRONGEST AND BRAVEST ANIMAL IN ANIMAL TOWN. RABBIT BOY SWORE TO ALWAYS USE HIS SPECIAL POWERS FOR GOOD. HE BECAME KNOWN TO EVERYONE AS **SUPER** RABBIT BOY!

Simon the Hedgehog tells Super Rabbit
Boy what happened. He tells him how King
Viking and his Robot Army stormed the
town and kidnapped poor Singing Dog.

4 THE ADVENTURE BEGINS

There are six levels between Super Rabbit Boy's home and the end of his adventure.

LEVEL 1: ANIMAL TOWN
LEVEL 2: SPLISH SPLASH SEA
LEVEL 3: SANDSTORM DESERT
LEVEL 4: CLOUDY HILLS
LEVEL 5: MOUNT BOOM
LEVEL 6: BOOM BOOM FACTORY

Each level is harder than the one before. Can Super Rabbit Boy beat them all?

Super Rabbit Boy springs into action on Level 1.

He finds some carrots to power up.

He hops from platform to platform.

And he jumps on King Viking's robots along the way. Jumping stops the robots!

Super Rabbit Boy completed the level!

LEVEL 2: SPLISH SPLASH SEA

Super Rabbit Boy eats a couple of carrots before jumping into the water.

Boing! Boing! Here I go!

Now Super Rabbit Boy is faced with many new dangers. He swims through small tunnels covered in spikes.

He dodges King Viking's Robo-Crabs and Robo-Fish as they try to grab and bite him.

SNAP!

He is getting tired, and he's running out of carrot power. Finally, the Exit is just ahead. Super Rabbit Boy is almost there when suddenly . . .

EXIT

A GIANT Robo-Fish has gobbled up Super Rabbit Boy! **Oh no!**

5 TRY AGAIN

2 LIVES LEFT!

Sigh. Let's go, Super Rabbit Boy!

Super Rabbit Boy is back at the beginning of
Level 2. He is a little confused.

Super Rabbit Boy swims ahead through
the level. But everything feels familiar.

None of the traps and tricks surprise him.
He seems to always know which way to go,
and which tunnels to take.

He is ready for every Robo-Crab and every
Robo-Fish.

Even the Giant Robo-Fish is no surprise.

Super Rabbit Boy swims to the Exit.

Hooray! Level 2 is finished!

LEVEL 3: SANDSTORM DESERT

Super Rabbit Boy sees a large, sandy desert as far as he can see. Super Rabbit Boy spots the Exit in the distance.

I can see the Exit already! This is going to be easy!

Super Rabbit Boy lands on the sand and starts running towards the Exit.

Poor Super Rabbit Boy! **Oh no!**

6 HOP OR SINK

Super Rabbit Boy is back at the beginning of Level 3. He's a little confused. Everything looks familiar. But he remembers something important.

Super Rabbit Boy jumps into action once again. This time, he hops all the way!

He hops from rock to rock.

He hops across the sand.

He hops on any Robo-Lizards that he finds in the desert.

Boing! Boing! This is fun!

37

Soon Super Rabbit Boy is almost at the Exit. He just needs to pass one last stretch of desert. The problem is it's full of swimming, munching, crunching, giant Robo-Snakes!

Oh bloop! Snakes!

Super Rabbit Boy does not like snakes. But he is very brave. He jumps straight ahead. The Robo-Snakes jump out at him. He dodges the first Robo-Snake.

He hops right past the second Robo-Snake.

He leaps quickly between the third and fourth Robo-Snakes.

And he bounces straight into the mouth of the fifth and final Robo-Snake!

LEVEL 3: SANDSTORM DESERT

Super Rabbit Boy is back at the beginning of Level 3. He is confused. But he quickly hops through the level towards the Robo-Snakes. Before Super Rabbit Boy faces the Robo-Snakes again, he sees a ledge.

Super Rabbit Boy jumps down. It's an entrance to a secret tunnel!

He runs through the tunnel.

Finally he is back out in the sunlight and right next to the Exit! The Robo-Snakes hiss as he waves good-bye.

With no lives left, Super Rabbit Boy enters Cloudy Hills.

LEVEL 4: CLOUDY HILLS

The platforms lead him up into the sky to Mount Boom. Boom Boom Factory sits at the very top of Mount Boom.

Super Rabbit Boy sees carrots. The more carrots he eats, the more super rabbit power he has. The more power he has, the higher he can jump.

He jumps from hill to platform.

From platform to hill.
Higher and higher.

Boing! Boing! Boing!

Super Rabbit Boy is almost at the end of the level. He just has to make it across one last very, very, **VERY** big gap.

Boing! Boing! BOING!
Here I go!

Luckily, he can jump really, really, **REALLY** high because of all the carrots he has eaten. He leaps over the very, very, **VERY** big gap . . . straight through the Exit.

UH-OH

LEVEL 5: MOUNT BOOM

Mount Boom is a very scary place. Super Rabbit Boy has no more lives left. But he is very, **VERY** brave! He leaps into action.

He jumps across lakes of lava!

He dodges fireballs!

He jumps from robot to robot!

Suddenly two giant robots jump out right in front of Super Rabbit Boy!

Robo-Basher Brother 1 swings his fist from the left. Super Rabbit Boy quickly hops out of the way.

Super Rabbit Boy lands in front of Robo-Basher Brother 2 who is already swinging his fist in from the right! He leaps once again, narrowly missing the giant robot's powerful punch.

He has avoided both punches.

Oh bloop! That was close!

But this time, Super Rabbit Boy lands right between the two robot brothers. They are swinging their fists at him from both directions!

BASH!

9 IF AT FIRST. . .

GAME START!

Super Rabbit Boy is back at Carrot Castle with Simon the Hedgehog.

Be careful, Super Rabbit Boy! King Viking's robots are everywhere.

Um, don't worry, Simon. Super Rabbit Boy is on the way. Again?

Super Rabbit Boy speeds through each level.
He swims past the Robo-Fish!

He runs through the secret tunnel!

He leaps over the very, very, **VERY** big gap!

Soon Super Rabbit Boy is back in front of the Robo-Basher Brothers in Level 5. He hops, runs, and leaps as hard as he can, but they beat him again . . .

and again . . .

 and again . . .

and again.

No matter how hard he tries, it always ends in . . .

59

Once again Super Rabbit Boy faces the Robo-Basher Brothers. But this time is different.

Super Rabbit Boy dodges every punch. He remembers their punching pattern! First he dodges a punch from the left, then from the right.

And with a quick double hop on to both robots' heads . . .

Super Rabbit Boy beats them at last! He is ready to move on to the final level.

10 LOST

LEVEL 6: BOOM BOOM FACTORY

Now Super Rabbit Boy enters the final level.
Inside the factory, it is very dark and scary!
Tunnels and paths lead in every direction.

Which way should I go?

Super Rabbit Boy goes from tunnel to tunnel and through door after door. But there is no sign of King Viking or Singing Dog.

This place is a maze! Where are they? Wait! What's that noise?

Super Rabbit Boy can hear a familiar sound coming down one of the tunnels. He heads towards it. The closer he gets, the louder the sound gets.

Right away, he dashes through the maze towards the source of the sound.

At long last, Super Rabbit Boy has found Singing Dog . . .

. . . with a dancing, smiling, and laughing
King Viking?

BATTLE TIME!

Suddenly, King Viking spots Super Rabbit Boy!
He stops dancing and Super Rabbit Boy laughs.

Ha! Ha! You stinker King Viking! I thought you didn't like music or dancing or having fun!

I don't like it! I DON'T! I DON'T! I don't like it, and if you think you are going to leave here with Singing Dog and tell anyone that I do . . .

Super Rabbit Boy has had enough of King Viking and his robots. He swam through traps, escaped Robo-Snakes, survived lava, and beat an entire army of super-mean robots. He is ready to finish this adventure once and for all.

He leaps in the air and hops on the head
of King Viking's Mega Robo-Viking Armour once.

Then twice.

Then three times.

The armour explodes with a big blast! King Viking is flung right through the roof of Boom Boom Factory!

Back in Animal Town, there is a big party to thank Super Rabbit Boy for saving Singing Dog. Singing Dog sings better than ever and everyone has lots and lots and LOTS of FUN!

Super Rabbit Boy has brought happiness back to Animal Town!

THOMAS FLINTHAM

has always loved to draw and tell stories, and now that is his job! He grew up in Lincoln, England, and studied illustration in Camberwell, London. He now lives by the sea with his dog, Ziggy, in Cornwall.

Thomas is the creator of AROUND THE WORLD COLOURING BOOK and illustrated the Izzy series by Pamela Butchart. PRESS START! is his first early chapter book series.

Some things Thomas likes include:

video games,

rainy days,

all kinds of books,

and yummy, yummy chocolate.

SUPER FUNSTON

START
SELECT

PRESS START!

How much do you know about

GAME ON, SUPER RABBIT BOY!?

What is it like to live in Animal Town?

Look at page 6. What are King Viking's plans?

How does Rabbit Boy turn into Super Rabbit Boy?

How does Super Rabbit Boy finally beat the Robo-Basher Brothers?

Look at page 18. What is Simon the Hedgehog saying? Draw Simon with a speech bubble. Then write one sentence of dialogue inside the bubble.

www.nosycrow.com